Géraldine Elschner was born in France. She studied German and Romance languages and trained as a librarian specializing in children's literature. Elschner has been translating children's books from German into French and writing their own stories for years. Today she lives in Heidelberg, Germany.

Alexandra Junge was born in Lüdinghausen, Germany. She studied illustration with a focus on children's book illustration at the Hamburg University of Applied Sciences and at the École supérieure des arts décoratifs in Strasbourg. She has been illustrating children's books since 2001. Her original pictures and illustrations have appeared in exhibitions in Italy and France. Alexandra Junge lives and works in Freiburg, Germany.

For my chic of March 21 — G. E.

Copyright © 2003 by Michael Neugebauer Verlag,
and imprint of NordSüd Verlag AG, CH-8050, Zürich, Switzerland.
First published in Switzerland under the title *Das Osterküken*.
English translation copyright © 2004 by NorthSouth Books, Inc., New York 10016.
Translated by Marianne Martens

First published in the United States, Great Britain, Canada, Australia, and New Zealand in 2004 by NorthSouth Books, Inc., an imprint of NordSüd Verlag AG, CH-8050 Zürich, Switzerland.
This edition published in 2022.

Distributed in the United States by NorthSouth Books, Inc., New York 10016.
Library of Congress Cataloging-in-Publication Data is available.
ISBN: 978-0-7358-4474-2 (trade edition)
1 3 5 7 9 · 10 8 6 4 2
Printed in Latvia by Livonia Print, Riga, 2021.
www.northsouth.com

The Easter Chick

By Géraldine Elschner • Illustrated by Alexandra Junge

Translated by Marianne Martens

NorthSouth

Hilda had laid the most beautiful egg, and she fussed over it lovingly. But she was getting a little worried. Weeks had passed, and still her baby hadn't hatched. Suddenly she heard a little voice. "Mother, when is Easter?" Hilda jumped up in shock. Who could be speaking to her?

"Please, Mother, please tell me. How many more days?"

Hilda couldn't believe it. The voice seemed to be coming from the egg.

"Un . . . un . . . until Easter?" Hilda sputtered. "Why, I'm not sure! I know Easter is in the spring. Sometimes it's in March, other times in April. Each year it changes."

"Oh, Mother, please find out for me," peeped the little chick. "The whole chicken coop keeps talking about how lovely Easter is, so I really wanted to hatch on Easter Sunday. I want to be an Easter chick."

"That is certainly an amazing idea," said Hilda, "but why not?" So off she went to find out.

First Hilda asked the dog. Then the cat. Then the cow. Then the pig, and finally the sheep. "When is Easter?" she asked. But no one knew the answer. Not even the bunnies. "Sorry, we're not Easter bunnies," they apologized. "Maybe Max can help you."

Max the owl lived in a tree behind the barn.
That night Hilda snuck out of the chicken coop
to ask Max about Easter.

"Of course I know when Easter is," said Max.
"If your little chick wants to hatch on Easter, three
things have to happen. First, she must wait for the
first day of spring. On that evening, I'll hoot once.
When you hear me, meet me by the barn."

Hilda ran back to her nest and told her
little chick what the owl had said.

"Oh, I can hardly wait!" said the little
chick impatiently.

Finally March 21 arrived and with it came spring.

That night, a sound awakened her from across the barnyard.

Whoooo hoooo!

Quickly Hilda ran to the big barn.

"Your little chick still needs to be patient," explained Max. "She will have to wait for the next full moon. On that night, I'll hoot two times. When you hear me, meet me by the barn."

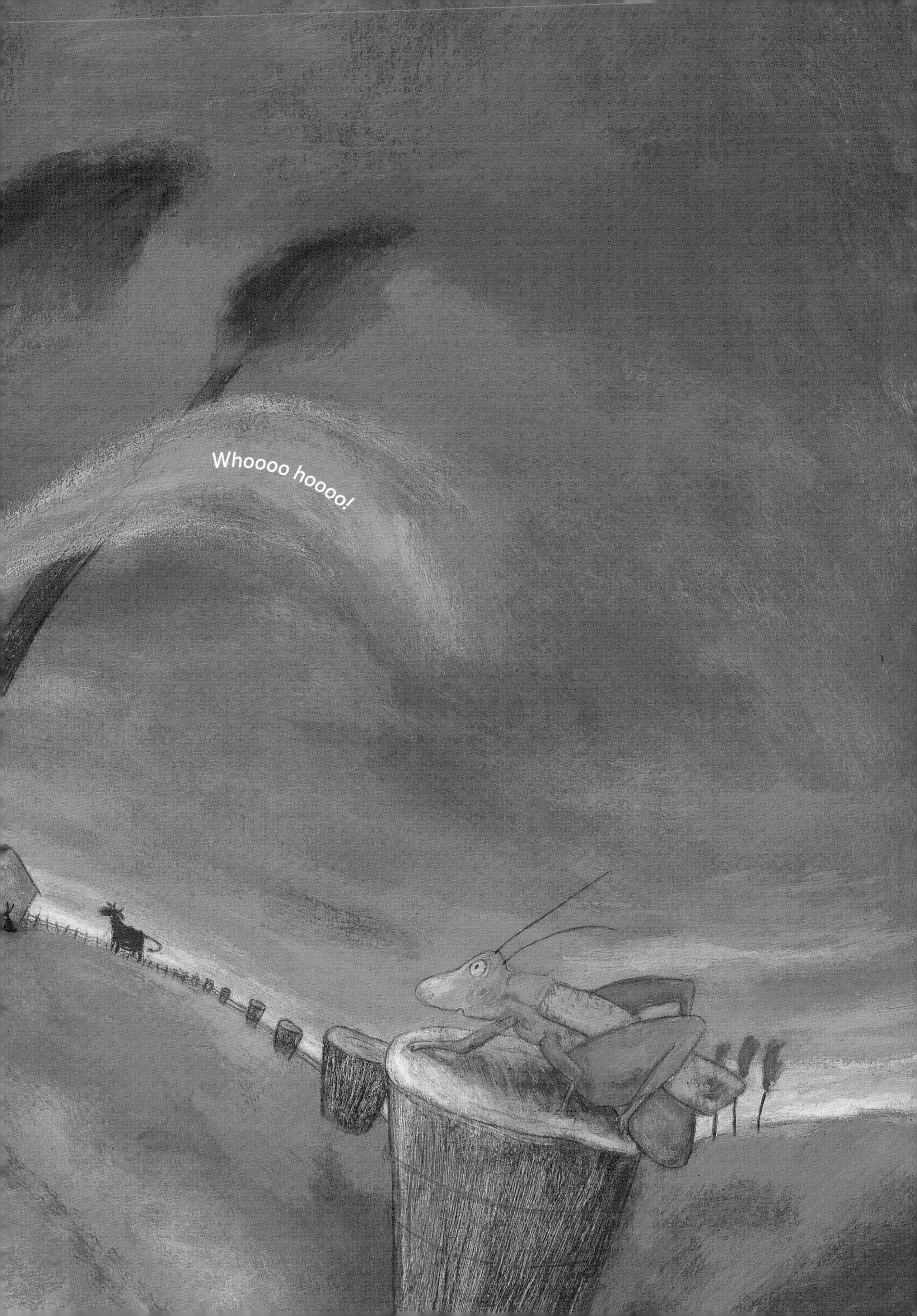
Whoooo hoooo!

The little chick grew more and more impatient.
"How will I know when the moon is full?" she said.
"I can't see anything from inside this egg."
So Hilda poked a tiny hole in the egg and stuck a piece
of straw in so that her baby could watch the moon.

At first the moon was thin and curved like a backward letter C.

Slowly it started to take the shape of a horn.

Every night it grew thicker and rounder.

"It won't be long before the full moon is here," said Hilda.

The little chick jumped for joy, making the egg wobble.

When the moon was finally full,
Hilda heard Max hooting again: *Whooo hoooo!*
Whooo hoooo! "Next Sunday will be Easter," said Max.
"Easter is always the first Sunday after the first
full moon that comes after the first day of spring.
"On the night before Easter, I'll hoot
three times. The next morning when the church bells
ring, it will be Easter, and your little chick can
finally hatch out of her egg."

The little chick counted down
the days:
Monday,
Tuesday,
Wednesday,
Thursday,
Friday.
On Saturday night, there were three
loud calls through the barnyard.
Whoooo hoooo!
Whoooo hoooo!
Whoooo hoooo!

On Easter morning, all the church bells started to ring at once.

"Here I come!" called the little chick, happily cracking out of her egg.

"Father! Mother! Come quickly!" called the farmer's children, who were looking for Easter eggs in the barn. "A little chick just hatched! On Easter Sunday! Isn't that amazing?"

Hilda and her little chick smiled at each other. It *was* pretty amazing at that!

Then the little chick headed outside
to admire the big, bright, beautiful world.
"HAPPY EASTER!" she called.
"HAPPY EASTER BIRTHDAY to me!"